SQUARE

by

Mac Barnett

&

Jon Klassen

CANDLEWICK PRESS

This is Square.

This is Square's secret cave.

Every day, Square goes down into his cave

and takes a block from the pile below the ground.

He pushes the block up and out of the cave.

He brings the block to the pile at the top of the hill.

This is his work.

One day while Square was doing his work,

Circle floated by.

"Square!" said Circle. "You are a genius!
I did not know you were a sculptor!"
"Ah, yes," said Square. "What is a sculptor?"

"A sculptor shapes blocks into art," said Circle.
"Ah, yes," said Square. "I see what you mean."
But he did not really see what she meant.

"This is a wonderful sculpture," said Circle.
"It looks just like you!"

Square looked at his block.
"Yes, I suppose it is wonderful."

"Now," said Circle, "you must do one of me."
"Oh," said Square.

"I will come back for it tomorrow! Good-bye, genius!"
"Circle," said Square, "I think I should tell you something."

But she was already gone.

"Oh dear dear dear," said Square.

He studied the block.

"I have to make this block look
like Circle," he said.

"Circle is perfect. So I must
make this perfect."

Square got to work shaping the block.

"Oh crumbs!" said Square. "This is not perfect!"

"Oh dirt!" said Square. "This is much worse."

He went back to work.

He worked and worked

and worked and worked.

"AAAH!" cried Square.

He had carved the whole block away.

There was nothing left.

He was surrounded by rubble.

"Whatever is the opposite of perfect,

that is what this is! I must stay up

all night and figure this out!"

Square fell asleep.

The next morning,
Square woke up wet.
He despaired.
"What have I done?
I push blocks.
I do not shape them.
I am not a genius."

"Hello, genius!" said Circle. "I am early!"

"Oh dear," whispered Square.

"Are you finished?" asked Circle.

"Oh yes," said Square. "I am finished."

Circle peered down.
"Oh my," she said.

It was beautiful.

It was beguiling.

"It is perfect," said Circle.

"It is?" asked Square.

"Yes," said Circle.

"You are a genius," said Circle.

But was he really?

For the Malks: Sylvie, Oliver, Alex, and Steve
M. B.

For Henry, who is perfect
J. K.

MAC BARNETT & JON KLASSEN
have made four books together: *Sam and Dave Dig a Hole,*
which won a Caldecott Honor and an E. B. White Read
Aloud Award; *Extra Yarn,* which won a Caldecott Honor, an
E. B. White Read Aloud Award, and a *Boston Globe–Horn
Book* Award; *Triangle;* and *Square,* which is the book you
are reading right now. They both live in California, but in
different cities. Jon's Canadian; Mac's not.